JUST WHAT I ALWAYS WANTED

Stories by Brilliant Authors

First published in Great Britain by Collins in 1998
Collins is an imprint of HarperCollins*Publishers* Ltd
77-85 Fulham Palace Road, Hammersmith, London, W6 8JB

1 3 5 7 9 8 6 4 2

ISBN 0 00 675364 7

Printed and bound in Great Britain by Caledonian International
Book Manufacturing Ltd, Glasgow G64

Just What I Always Wanted

Stories by Brilliant Authors

Collins

An imprint of HarperCollinsPublishers

THE BUTTERFLY LION
by Michael Morpurgo

Bertie rescues an orphaned white lion cub from the African veld. They are inseparable until Bertie is sent to boarding school in England and the lion is sent to a circus. Bertie swears that one day they will see one another again, but it is the butterfly lion which ensures that their friendship will never be forgotten.

"*The Butterfly Lion* is unique among animals and books, and will touch all hearts – both young and old." Virginia McKenna, Born Free Foundation.

0 00675103 2

£3.50

SPACEBABY
Henrietta Branford

Warning!
The Earth is losing weight.
Everything's falling up instead of down.
Gravity's gone wrong!

Can Spacebaby fix gravity before we all drop off the World?
A computer game called Zucchini holds the key. Hector agrees to help, but Hector's no genius on computers, Hector is a dog! Spacebaby and his friends race to save the Earth, but Silas Stoatwarden has other ideas... "I want the alien and I want him now!"

"A delicious book, fast and funny and full of wonderful characters." The Guardian

THE UPSIDE-DOWN MICE

AND OTHER ANIMAL STORIES
Compiled by Jane Merer

The next night when the mice came out of their holes they were still joking and laughing about what they had seen the night before. But now, when they looked up at the ceiling, they stopped laughing very suddenly.

Roald Dahl's tale of how one man outwits a load of crafty mice, spearheads this collection of animal stories published in aid of The Malcolm Sargent Cancer Fund for Children. Entertaining, funny, or moving, the stories demonstrate why the authors are among the best of British writers for children – Elisabeth Beresford, Colin Dann, Roald Dahl, Dick King-Smith, Rose Impey, Penelope Lively, E. Nesbit, Brian Patten and Philippa Pearce.

Order Form

To order direct from the publishers, just make a list of the titles you want and fill in the form below:

Name ....

Address ....

....

....

Send to: Dept 6, HarperCollins Publishers Ltd, Westerhill Road, Bishopbriggs, Glasgow G64 2QT.

Please enclose a cheque or postal order to the value of the cover price, plus:

UK & BFPO: Add £1.00 for the first book, and 25p per copy for each additional book ordered.

Overseas and Eire: Add £2.95 service charge. Books will be sent by surface mail but quotes for airmail despatch will be given on request.

A 24-hour telephone ordering service is available to holders of Visa, MasterCard, Amex or Switch cards on 0141- 772 2281.

Collins
An *Imprint of HarperCollins Publishers*

"My dad went with her. Over two hundred he brought back. Badly wounded, some of them. Sea was rough as hell, s'what my dad said." He looked up at the sky. "Don't much like the look of this weather. Blowing up a bit. We'll fish a few minutes more, and then we'll head home."

The sky above was low and grey and heavy. The sea was whipping the waves into a frenzy all around us.

At that moment I felt a tug on my line and reeled in. Two mackerel! But I couldn't get them off the hook. Mr Pender reached over to help me. The boat lurched violently and we fell together onto the deck. When I got up, he didn't. I turned him over, but his eyes weren't open. I shouted at him. I shook him. There was a red mark on his forehead and blood coming from it. Then the engine mackerel and chips, with lashings of tomato sauce.

Mr Pender showed me how to let the line out till I felt it touch the bottom. Then I'd reel it in slowly, to entice the fish. I caught a small pollock, which I unhooked and threw back, and a lot of seaweed. Nothing else. Mr Pender fished beside me. For an hour or more we didn't catch a thing. *Nemo* rolled in the swell, the engine ticking over.

"*Nemo* was one of the small ships, y'know," said Mr Pender.

"What d'you mean?" I asked.

"Dunkirk, during the War, when the army was trapped on the beaches in France. Quarter of a million men. They sent over every boat they could find to pick them up. Several out of Scilly. *Nemo* is the only one left.

My present from Mum was a morning of mackerel fishing on *Nemo*, Mr Pender's launch. Mr Pender would take me all on my own.

Like lots of visitors, I'd been out in *Nemo* before. She's one of the open blue and white boats that take you to look at seals off the Eastern Islands, or puffins off Annet. Her engine purred and throbbed as we cleared St Mary's harbour and turned towards St Martin's.

"We'll find mackerel off Great Arthur," said Mr Pender, pushing back his sailor's cap. "Be a bit of a swell out there. You don't get seasick, do you?"

I shook my head and hoped.

I'd been fishing once before and loved it. You could catch wrasse or pollock, but what I was really after was mackerel. My favourite meal in all the world is grilled

MACKEREL AND CHIPS

A month ago we were on the Isles of Scilly again for our holidays.

"Make a wish, Leah," said Mrs Pender, who keeps the bed and breakfast where we stay. My birthday. Ten years old. I blew out the candles on the cake and cut it slowly, gazing out at the lifeboat in St Mary's Bay, the same lifeboat I could see from my bedroom window every morning, every evening. I wish, I said inside my head, I wish I could go out in the lifeboat, just once.

"Tell, tell," cried Eloise, my little sister, pulling at me. But I told no-one.

MACKEREL AND CHIPS

BY

MICHAEL MORPURGO

Illustrated by Jon Riley

CONTENTS

stopped and the boat was wallowing, helpless in the waves. When I stood up I saw the rocks of the Eastern Isles looming closer and closer. There was no boat in sight, no-one to help. I couldn't work the boat all by myself. I had to wake Mr Pender, I had to.

When I turned back to him again there was a man crouching over him, a young man in khaki uniform, his arm in a sling, his head bandaged.

"Don't you worry, girl," he said, smiling up at me. "He'll be all right. Needs a doctor. You cover him up with the tarpaulin, keep him warm. I'll get the engine going. Don't want *Nemo* on the rocks, do we? Not after all she's done, all she's been through. Saved a lot of lives, she did."

The engine would not start at all at first. It just coughed and spluttered.

"Come on, *Nemo*," said the soldier, "get your skates on. Those rocks are looking awful sharp and awful hungry."

Mr Pender still wasn't moving. The engine roared suddenly to life. I looked out. We had our stern to the rocks and were heading out into clear open water.

"Take the helm!" the soldier called, beckoning me over. "I'm not much good, not with one arm."

Nemo ploughed through the sea at full throttle, the soldier beside me steadying the wheel with his good hand whenever it needed it. The spray came over the bows and showered us as *Nemo* rode over the crests of the waves and crashed down into the troughs.

"Just like it was at Dunkirk," said the soldier, his head back and laughing in the wind. "We made it then, we'll make it now. Look out for rocks, girl."

Only when we turned into the shelter of St Mary's harbour and the soldier pulled back the throttle did we stop tossing and turning.

"Beach her by the lifeboat slipway," he said, pointing. "And then we'll get a doctor for Mr Pender."

I steered a course through the anchored yachts as best I could, until *Nemo* ground up on the beach and came to a jolting stop, the engine still ticking over.

There were people running down the beach towards us, shouting at us, then climbing up into the boat. Someone was crouching over Mr Pender. Someone else was on the radio calling for an ambulance.

I tried to tell them what had happened.

"What soldier?" they said. But when I looked around for the soldier, he was gone.

The doctor examined me in the hospital. I told her about the soldier. I wasn't making much sense, she said. But I'd be fine. I was just a little exhausted, that's all.

"Bravest girl in the world," said Mr Pender later. "Saved the *Nemo*, saved me."

"It was the soldier," I told him; but just like the doctor, he wasn't listening.

I had mackerel and chips that evening and tomato sauce, lashings of it. Eloise pinched most of the chips. Well, she would.

The next day, when the storm had passed, the Scilly lifeboat took us all out on a special trip as a reward – for my bravery, they said. As I passed the Eastern Isles, I made a wish. I wished I could see my soldier again, just once, to thank him. But I never did. Some wishes come true, I suppose. Others don't.

LITTLE GREEN MEN

BY

JEAN URE

Illustrated by Dave McTaggart

LITTLE GREEN MEN

Lisa said, "Little green *men*?"

"Three of 'em!"

"*Green*?"

"Pea green," said Andrew.

Lisa narrowed her eyes. Pippa plucked at her elbow.

"L— Lisa— "

"We didn't want to scare you off or anything," said Tom, "but that was the field they came down in." He pointed over the garden fence, towards Longshaw Meadow. "Right over there, by the oak trees."

"We just thought we ought to warn

you." Andrew said it carelessly. "Seeing as you're going to be spending the night out here."

Pippa chewed nervously on her bottom lip. She had never been as keen as Lisa at the idea of camping out in the garden. But they had to do it, because Lisa had said so. It was a dare.

The boys had done it last night, just to prove that there was nothing to it. Now it was the girls' turn. Lisa drew herself up.

"I'm not going to be bothered by any old space ship! It's only a story anyway."

"That's what you think," said Tom.

Pippa swallowed. "Did you s–say your uncle s–saw it?"

"Yup." Andrew nodded. "He was driving home one night and he saw it come down and these three little green men got out."

"What did they d–do?" said Pippa.

Oh dear! Pippa was so impressionable. Tell her there were goblins having a tea party under the gooseberry bush and she'd believe you.

"They surrounded him," said Tom.

"Touched at him," said Andrew.

"Gave him this thing."

"What sort of thing?"

"Little pink stone," said Tom.

"With writing on it," said Andrew.

"Oh, *really*?" Lisa put her hands on her hips. "And what did it say exactly?"

"He doesn't know. He's never been able to read it. It's all in this alien language."

"So why hasn't he taken it to a museum?"

"'Cos he knows they'd just laugh at him."

"No-one ever believes people when they say they've seen space ships. We were kind of hoping," said Andrew, "that we'd have seen one last night."

"That's why we told you," said Tom. "One's due just about any time now."

"How do you know?" scoffed Lisa.

"They told him. My uncle. They said they send one every ten years, just to, like, check up on us."

"Oh, yes?" Lisa curled her lip. "Spoke English to him, did they?"

"Spoke in his head," said Andrew. He tapped his forehead. "It's called telepathy."

"Ha, ha, very funny," said Lisa.

"You can laugh if you want," said Tom. "But it could be pretty scary. We just thought we ought to warn you."

"Don't you worry about us," said

Lisa. "The bet is still on... fifty pence each if we do what we've said we'll do!"

"Think they will?" said Andrew, as the two girls went off.

"Not a chance!" Tom sniggered. "You wait till it gets dark!"

Pippa was scared of the dark. She'd only agreed to carry out the dare because Lisa had bullied her. Lisa was so butch! Always wanting to put the boys in their place.

"You surely don't *believe* what they were saying?" said Lisa. "They were just trying to wind us up. Trying to put us off. They don't want to have to pay us fifty pence. There aren't any such things as space ships."

"Oh, well, no, of course, I know *that*," said Pippa.

All the same...

It was still a bit scary. Even Lisa hadn't realised quite how goose-pimply it could make you feel, all by yourselves in a small tent in the middle of the garden in the pitch black at the dead of night, and help, help! What on earth was that? Was it the wind? Was it the rain? Was it an earthquake?

"L–Lisa," quavered Pippa.

Lisa gritted her teeth. "We are not giving up *now*. If they can do it, so can we!"

Next day, in the playground, the four of them met up.

"Well?" said Tom with a grin. "How'd it go?"

"Fine," said Lisa. "Nothing to it."

Tom and Andrew exchanged glances. "You've got your mum's signature, like we agreed?"

"Got my dad's, an' all," said Lisa. She handed Tom a piece of paper. It was signed by her parents:

This is to certify that Lisa and Pippa spent last night sleeping in the garden.

"Oh, and we got this for you, as well," said Lisa. "Give it to him, Pips."

Pippa put her hand in her pocket and held out a small round object. Tom eyed it, suspiciously. "What's this?"

"Little pink stone," said Lisa. "With *alien* writing."

Tom scowled. "What are you on about?"

"It came," said Lisa.

"The space ship," said Pippa.

"Landed right there in the field."

"Just like you said it would."

"So now you owe us fifty pence."

"*Each*."

The girls linked arms and set off across the playground.

"Oh! And by the way," said Lisa. She turned and smiled, sweetly. "Your uncle got one thing wrong... It wasn't little green men. It was little green women!"

THE ELEPHANTS' REVENGE

BY

JAMILA GAVIN

Illustrated by Simone Lai

THE ELEPHANTS' REVENGE

While the engineer built a railway, his daughter, Shanta, watched elephants on the river bank. They came out of the jungle to drink and bathe.

One day, she noticed a disturbance. The herd encircled a she-elephant, showering her with cooling dust, tenderly nudging something at her feet.

"It's a new-born elephant!" exclaimed Shanta.

The baby rolled weakly. Mother hooked its body with her trunk. Baby must get to its feet as soon as possible; there were tigers and hyenas, who would love to gobble it up. The whole herd shielded the calf with their huge, loving bodies.

The girl rushed back to tell her father. "I've just seen a baby..."

"Not now, dear, I'm tired. We have a big day tomorrow. The railway and the bridge are complete and the minister himself is arriving for the grand opening on a special train. You and I will be the first to try out our new line. Go to bed."

The next day, the engineer and his daughter went to the railway station in their best clothes. There were flags and flowers and brass bands.

From the platform, Shanta saw the elephants by the river. The baby wobbled on its feet; the herd helped it into the water.

"Daddy! Look! There's the baby

elephant I saw born yesterday. I wish I could take it home with me."

"I'll see what I can do," said the engineer. He went over and had a word with the station master, who spoke to the head of the village. He summoned the local elephant-keeper, the mahout.

The mahout shook his head. "It isn't right to take a baby from its mother so soon."

"Obey my orders!" snapped the head of the village. So the mahout went into the herd, gently talking to them, until he had reached the little one. The mother elephant swayed, agitated. She churned up the dust with her huge feet, but she didn't hurt the mahout when he dropped a rope round the baby's neck and led it to the station.

There was a great commotion going

on. The minister had arrived and was cutting the scarlet ribbon.

"I now declare this railway open!"

Everyone clapped. The band played. The baby elephant trumpeted in distress. Shanta threw her arms around it.

"Dear little baby. Don't cry," she said. "I'll look after you."

The engineer led the baby up the platform. The mahout then noticed that the herd had left the river. Where had they gone? Then he saw them pounding towards the station.

"Shoo, shoo!" yelled the station master. "Go away!"

The elephants were charging to the station and heading straight for the barrier.

"Get these elephants out of here!"

"They've come for their baby," said

the mahout. "Nothing will make them go until they have him back."

"Nonsense," said the station master. "Get rid of them. They're spoiling the show."

Majestically, the train pulled into the station. People crowded into the carriages. The engineer and his daughter got into the VIP carriage, along with the minister. The baby elephant was put into the guard's van. How the creature howled.

"He wants his mummy!" cried Shanta. "Should we let him go?"

"Of course not," said her father. "It's only an animal. It will soon forget."

The cheering turned to screams. Elephants pounded up the platform. They reached the guard's van and smashed it open. Mother elephant trumpeted joyfully as baby tumbled out. The engine driver tried to back his train up, but the elephants rampaged on to the line and tore down the bridge, piece by piece.

They moved from carriage to carriage as though they were searching for someone. Eventually, they found the minister, the engineer and his daughter. The elephants smashed open the doors and dragged them out. Then they carried them down to the edge of the bridge to hurl them into the water.

First, the elephants threw in the engineer and the minister. Finally, the mother elephant picked up Shanta. The mahout stepped forward and spoke gently into the mother elephant's ear. She lowered the child into his arms.

"We shouldn't have taken the baby away from his mother," whispered the

girl. "You can't blame them for being angry."

As the engineer and the minister clambered from the river, sopping wet, the elephants turned and walked back to the jungle. In their midst was the baby elephant, sheltered from the outside world by the huge bodies of its protectors.

WORLD CUP FEVER

BY

MICHAEL HARDCASTLE

Illustrated by Ann Johns

WORLD CUP FEVER

"**W**e can't miss the World Cup Final!" Matthew protested. "I've waited years to see it."

"I can cheerfully miss anything to do with football," replied his mum. "Anyway, you've seen lots lately. There's been nothing else on TV. So you can sacrifice one match. Our holiday comes first."

"But Mum..." Matthew protested.

"That's enough, Matthew," replied Mrs Buxton firmly. "It might be different if one of the UK sides were playing. But they aren't."

Patiently, Matthew waited until she and his sister Gemma had gone to the supermarket before telephoning his favourite teacher, Miss McCormack.

"Hi, Matt, good to hear you," she said. "Been enjoying the Brazilian back heels, the Italian flair and the German oomph? Great, isn't it?"

"Yeah, but..."

"Sorry your favourite player's injured. Still, he can always watch the Final on TV from his hospital bed, I suppose."

"Yeah," Matthew agreed, hardly listening. "Only thing is, we're off on holiday tomorrow. Mum booked it ages ago. Worst timing in the world."

"Oh, Matt, I am sorry. My boyfriend and I are going away too, to Paris. I've made sure they've got a TV in our room though!"

Matt's heart sank again, but he still managed to wish Miss McCormack a happy holiday.

When it rained on the first day as the family headed for the beach, Matt knew the holiday was going to be a disaster. Instead of returning to the caravan (which at least had a TV) Mrs Buxton insisted on dragging Matt and Gemma around the shops.

Then, on the second day, they returned from the bowling alley to find the caravan had been broken into – and the TV set was missing.

"I can't believe it!" Matthew wailed. "We can't live without a TV to see the Final."

"Well I can," his mum said firmly. "It'll be on the radio. Listen to that and use your imagination."

"But there won't be another Final for four years. I'll die if I miss it."

"Rubbish, Matthew! Nobody dies from not watching a football match. They don't even faint."

Matthew went out, thinking furiously. He juggled a ball, up on to this neck, holding it between his shoulder blades, dropping it on to this heel to flick it up again for a volley against the farmer's wall.

Would the farmer be watching the Final?
he wondered. No chance, thought
Matthew. He remembered the grizzled
old man warning Mum not to let anyone
kick a ball near his cows in case their milk
dried up. So he'd had it, unless...

Two hours before the Final, Matthew
fainted. He'd never done it before and his
mum was alarmed. She phoned for an
ambulance.

"How are you feeling?" the doctor
asked as Matthew opened his eyes.
Matthew tried to think of a word to
guarantee himself an overnight stay in
hospital.

"Woozy," he replied. That did it.

"Right, we'd better keep you in
overnight, Matthew," said the doctor.
"Just for observation. You can't be too

careful. Come on, hop aboard."

Matthew got into the waiting wheelchair and was whisked away down a labyrinth of corridors by a hospital orderly. His mother followed anxiously behind. They turned one corner after another for what seemed an eternity before a huge pair of doors loomed.

Pushing through with a clang, a nurse swooped out of the office to greet the party. Matthew's mouth fell open. There at the end of the ward was the most wonderful sight – the biggest colour TV he had ever seen, playing the World Cup signature tune. The Final was just about to begin.

"I hope you'll be very comfortable here," said the nurse, kindly.

Matthew smiled. "I think I'll be just fine."

HUNT THE BABY

BY

JACQUELINE WILSON

Illustrated by Julian Mosedale

HUNT THE BABY

Who's there? *Boo.* Boo who? *No need to cry, it's only a joke!*

I'm Elsa. I'm always telling jokes. I drive everyone daft.

I live in the Star Hotel. It's ever so posh. Don't get the wrong idea. We're not rich. We're so poor we lost our house and had to live crowded into one room in a truly crummy hotel, but then there was a fire (I raised the alarm and got to be so famous I was on television!) so for the moment we've been re-housed. Well, re-hoteled.

In the Star Hotel we feel like stars and

we all go twinkle-twinkle. Even my stepdad, Mack. He hasn't smacked me once since we've been here. My mum doesn't go to bed during the day any more. My little sister Pippa hasn't wet the bed once. But my baby brother Hank hasn't half caused a lot of trouble!

Hank doesn't cry much. He eats heaps. He goes to sleep straight away when you tuck him up in his bed. By the way, what animal goes to sleep with its shoes on? *A horse!* Hank goes to sleep in his bed, yes. But he doesn't stay there. You can tuck him up really tight so he can hardly turn over and then you can cage him in – and yet when you wake up in the morning and look in his bed... he's gone! You have to play Hunt Little Hank: under our beds, in the bathroom, in the wardrobe. Once he got right out the door

and down the corridor before we caught up with him. He can't even walk yet, but he's a champion crawler.

He's never been properly lost though – apart from the Sunday we went to this car boot sale. Hey, what birds hover over people lost in the desert? *Luncheon vultures!*

It was a really super-duper sale, with

ice-cream vans and sweet stalls and a roundabout for little kids and heaps of people selling clothes and videos and T-shirts and toys. Mum spotted this fantastic sparkly top and started trying it on. She told me to watch Hank. Mack took Pippa off to get ice-creams. Aha – what did the baby ghost say when he wanted his favourite food? *I scream!* I dashed after Mack to make sure mine had a chocolate flake and then I turned back to Hank in his buggy and... you've guessed it. He'd slipped his reins and scarpered.

I searched everywhere. No Hank. Mum ran round calling him, stopping everyone to ask if they'd seen a baby boy. Nobody had. We started to panic. Mack and Pippa came back with the ice-creams and Mack got mega-miffed with me and I thought maybe I was going to get smacked after all. No-one felt like eating their ice-creams and they trickled down Mack's arms. My tears were trickling too because it looked like Hank was really lost this time.

I tried hard to work out where in the world he'd got to. Where would he make for? Had he wanted an ice-cream? What about sweets from the stall?

I whirled round, trying to spot him. Round and round about. Hey! The roundabout!

I was right! Hank was sitting up straight in this little toy train on the roundabout, grinning and gurgling gleefully.

"He must have climbed up all by himself," said the man in charge of the roundabout. "Well, he might as well have a good ride now he's here."

We were so happy to have found him we all had a ride. Mum climbed in the train with Hank and hugged him hard even though she told him how bad he was to run – well, crawl – away. Mack clambered on to a big pink elephant with Pippa on his lap. How do you get down off an elephant? *You can't. You get it off a swan!*

I sat on a horse with a golden mane and played cowboys. Maybe I'll have to learn how to use a lasso sometime.

Now that might be a way of capturing my bad baby brother Hank if he makes another escape attempt! OK, one last joke. Why did the cowboy get into trouble? *Because he couldn't stop horsing around.* That's me, all right!

JOEY AND THE DUTCH DESTROYER

BY

BRIAN JACQUES

Illustrated by Julie Anderson

JOEY AND THE DUTCH DESTROYER

Whumpity clumpity clatter bang thump! Mr Angelo called out as the ten-year-old boy thundered downstairs from the flat above his butcher shop.

"Hey, Joey, you gotta five pounds ninety-nine now?"

Joey Evans jumped the last four stairs and skidded into the shop. Opening a chubby fist under the butcher's nose, he showed him the crumpled five pound note and a single pound coin.

"He-hah! See, Mr Angelo. Six pounds, 'nuff to get my mum her present. Only three days to Christmas now. Postie been yet?"

The butcher shrugged. "One time early on he comes, he be back later. Your mamma still waitin' for her letter?"

Joey folded the money back tight into his fist. "Don't worry, Grandad an' Grandma will write. I told Mum that if the postman doesn't bring the letter then Santa Claus will."

Mr Angelo began taking turkeys out of the refrigerator. "So, whatta your mamma say about that, eh?"

Joey pulled a face, shrugging just like Mr Angelo did. "She said Santa an' one-parent families don't mix these days. When her letter arrives she'll cheer up, bet she'll believe in Santa Claus then."

Joey dashed off, anxious to get into town to buy his mother's gift. Mr Angelo shouted after him:

"That'sa right, Joey boy, you make

your mamma happy. Go easy now, don't lose that money, be careful crossi' the roads, eh!"

But Joey was gone, a podgy little figure racing down the street.

Mr Angelo addressed a frozen turkey. "Christmas no fun for a kid with no pappa, eh, but Joey's a good boy, doesn't get inna trouble an' loves his mamma, whatta you think, eh?"

The frozen turkey never answered him. It was a cold silent type.

Joey ran down the street breathing in the festive feeling. Christmas trees outside shops, fairy lights in windows and Yuletide music drifting out into the grey Tuesday city morning. It had been a long hard struggle, saving the money for his mum's Christmas present, but he had done it. They had first seen the scarf in the window of Bettafashions at the shopping centre, it was real silk, reduced from seven ninety-nine to five ninety-nine. Draped across a leather handbag the scarf looked like a miniature waterfall of soft green and hazy gold.

He saw in his mother's eyes that she longed to have it, even though she spoke aloud denying the fact.

"Five ninety-nine, hmph! Very pretty, but not at that price."

Clasping his mum's hand, Joey had whispered, "Maybe Santa Claus'll get it for you."

She tugged him away from the window towards the supermarket. "Santa Claus is all very well when you're young."

Now Joey had the money he was

determined to prove to his mum that Santa Claus existed. Fifteen minutes' hard running would take him to the shopping centre and Bettafashions.

Rushing past the arcade, Joey did not see the booted foot sticking out until too late. He tripped, opening his hands as the pavement came up. The money spilled on the pavement. Rolling over quickly, he grabbed it – but not fast enough. Jeggzer and Bullet had seen it. They were bigger and older than Joey, fatter, too.

Jeggzer laughed. It sounded like a rhinoceros with laryngitis. "Lend us six quid, we'll pay yer back after Christmas!"

Joey scrambled to his feet, knowing that if he refused the bullying demand the pair would take his money anyhow. It called for some quick thinking. Glancing over their shoulders, he yelled out, "Set the dog on 'em, constable!"

Jeggzer and Bullet turned momentarily. It was all Joey needed. He was off like a shot down a side street. The bullies were right after him. He heard their boots pounding behind, rage adding speed after falling for a little kid's bluff. Along streets, across alleys and down back cracks they chased him, getting closer by the second. Joey's eyes were wide. Breathing raggedly he ran onward, his legs rapidly beginning to tire.

Suddenly Joey found himself up a cul-de-sac, between two rows of back entrances lined with dustbins. He had run himself into a dead end, he was trapped! Red-faced but triumphant, the bullies closed in. It was Bullet who laughed this time, he sounded even worse than Jeggzer, like a breathless bulldog choking on a sausage.

Joey's heart sank as Bullet grabbed him by the collar.

"Gotcher! Now 'and over that money, kid!"

A side door swung open and a tiny, white-bearded man emerged from the rear of Murphy's Gym. He was carrying two well-filled black plastic rubbish bags. Setting them down, he pointed a stubby finger at the bullies.

"You two, leave der boy alone, go away now!"

Jeggzer grinned scornfully. "Beat it, Grandpop, 'fore y'get 'urt."

The little old man winked at Jeggzer, his eyes twinkling. "I don't get hurted, sonny. Mebbe you do if you don't let der boy go."

Bullet released Joey and joined Jeggzer. Both of them turned on the old man. "We'll teach yer t'mind your own business!"

They dived at him. Joey could hardly believe what happened next. The old fellow moved like a blur. Dropping to the floor, he rolled between his attackers, jumping up behind them as if propelled by springs. Before either bully could move he nipped the sides of their necks in his fingers and walked away from them without a backward glance. Smiling broadly through his thick white beard he bowed to Joey. "We go now, ja?"

Jeggzer and Bullet stood frozen like two statues, surprise pasted on their ugly faces, unable to move a muscle. Joey stepped around the two rigid bodies as he made for the alley mouth. "What happened, why are they stuck like that?"

The little old man wrinkled his red nose mischievously. "Huh, dey be alright in about ten minutes or so. I was gentle mit dem."

He pulled out a faded copy of *Grapple* magazine and leafed through it. "Here, dis is me, nineteen forty-seven."

Joey stared at the creased photograph. It showed the old man but much younger, black-bearded, standing in a fighting pose. Joey read aloud from the page:

"'*European wrestling champion wins Empire title. The Dutch Destroyer Iron Claus stripped Freddy Anaconda, the Birmingham Battler, of his British Empire title in one round with his famous Iron Claus hold.*'"

Joey handed the magazine back as he explained. "I was going to buy my mum a scarf for Christmas. They were after the money I'd saved up. I would've lost it but for you, Mr Claus."

Iron Claus patted Joey's head, even though he only stood an inch or so taller than him. "You a good boy, go now, buy your momma her gift. I go back and talk to those two about being nice at Christmas, ja? Go now."

✳✳✳✳

It was six pounds twenty-four to have the scarf packed in a special box with ribbon on it. However, the lady still only charged Joey five ninety-nine, because he told her he only had six pounds to buy his mum's present.

Things were being packed when Joey arrived back at the flat. The letter had arrived. They were going to live with Grandad and Grandma in Australia, by the shore and the sea, where the sun always shone. Holding the box behind his back, Joey grinned confidently at his mum.

"Mr Angelo said that you called the postman Santa Claus."

Joey's mum looked as if she were about to cry, but happy. "Don't believe Mr Angelo, he talks to turkeys. Still, who knows, maybe there is a Santa Claus."

Joey fingered the curling ribbons on the top of the box. "Believe me, Mum, there is a Santa Claus, honest. I met his brother today, he's called Iron Claus, looks just like Santa."

Joey's mum laughed then, it sounded just like Christmas. "Iron Claus, indeed, what'll you think of next, Joey?"

Taking the one penny change from his six pounds, Joey pressed it into his mother's hand and said with a straight face, "I think you'd better get this changed into Australian money, Mum."

OLYMPIC MARATHON

BY

MORRIS GLEITZMAN

Illustrated by Sami Sweeten

OLYMPIC MARATHON

The Twenty-seventh Summer Olympics arrive in Australia – four years early!

"Manchester," I pleaded softly. "Please, let it be Manchester."

Hoppy, my pet wallaby, stared at me as if I was mad, but I didn't care.

"Manchester," I moaned desperately, "or Beijing."

I held my breath.

Hoppy held his.

The bloke on the telly announced that the Olympic Games in the year 2000 had been awarded to... Sydney.

Australia went bananas.

In our lounge room and across our town and up and down the state and right round the country people leapt out of their chairs and whooped with joy and hugged each other and their pets.

All except me.

I just sat there and watched Dad try to do a delighted cartwheel and crash into the electric bug zapper.

"Here we go," I muttered to Hoppy. "We're cactus, now."

It started that evening.

I was drying up after tea when I heard Dad's voice behind me.

"A superb effort from the eleven-year-old," he said. "Look at that wiping action. This could be his personal best on the saucepan with lid."

I sighed.

OK, Dad does a pretty good sports commentator's voice for an abattoir worker, but all I could think of was the one thousand nine hundred and twenty-seven days to go till the Sydney Olympics.

"But wait!" yelled Dad. "Look at this burst of speed from his nine-year-old rival. Fourteen point six three seconds for the non-stick frying pan. That's got to be close to a world record if she can get it on the shelf without dropping it."

Sharon, my sister, rolled her eyes.

He was still at it two hours later when we were cleaning our teeth.

"It's Sharon, Sharon's holding on to her lead around the back teeth, but wait, she's slipped, her brush has slipped, oh no, this is a tragedy for the plucky youngster, she's missed a molar and Brendan has taken the lead, he's streaking home along the front ones, it's gold, it's gold, it's gold for Australia!"

Before we could remind Dad that shouting before bed gives kids nightmares, he herded us out into the backyard.

Sitting under the clothes hoist were three banana crates, the middle one taller than the others.

"The winners' podium," announced Dad.

We stared, mouths open.

Dad had always been mad about sport, but he'd never gone this far.

Weak with shock, we allowed ourselves to be led up on to the podium, where Sharon received the silver medal for teeth cleaning and I was awarded the gold for not dropping the frying pan.

Mum stuck her head out the back door.

"Bedtime, you kids," she said. "It's eight-fifteen."

"Crossing now to the back door," shouted Dad, "to witness a true champion in action."

Before she knew it, Mum was on the podium having an old beer bottle top on a ribbon hung round her neck for telling the right time.

****

Over the next days, gold medals were won at our place for potato peeling, TV watching, ironing, getting up in the morning, pet care, closing the fridge door, vacuuming, chess, whistling, putting socks on, toast scraping, yawning, homework, head scratching, microwave operation, hiccups, sleeping, nose picking, sitting down, standing up, walking, standing still, begging a parent to stop, and chucking a plastic strainer at a parent.

"Love," Mum said to Dad as he was hanging another bottle top round her neck (spin dryer repairs), "don't you think you're taking this a bit far?"

"Over to the spoilsports' stadium," said Dad, "where it looks like another gold for Australia!"

As the days turned into weeks, we all

wanted to scream.

Finally Mum did. "That's it!" she yelled. "If I hear another mention of medals, Olympics or personal best time in the loo, I'll kill someone!"

Dad muttered something under his breath about gold, gold, gold for getting cranky, then did what he always did when Mum blew her stack.

Took us to visit Uncle Wal.

Uncle Wal lives three hours away on a sheep farm.

It's a really boring trip because the land's flat and scrubby, the road's dead straight and you hardly ever see another car. Plus, when you get there, Uncle Wal hasn't even got a telly.

But this trip wasn't boring.

Half-an-hour up the track we ran out of petrol.

"It's a gold for Australia," said Sharon, "for forgetting to fill the car up."

Dad glared at her.

We waited for an hour.

No cars.

Finally, Dad got sick of giving us medals for waiting and set off on foot back to the petrol station in town.

For the next hour me and Sharon just enjoyed the silence.

Then I started to wish I had something to read.

I read the car manual, the soft drink cans on the floor, and all the print on the dashboard, including the numbers.

Which is where I saw something very interesting.

I showed Sharon.

Then we saw a cloud of dust heading towards us.

It was Mrs Garwick from school in her van.

Soon we were speeding back to town.

After a bit I saw Dad in the distance, trudging along.

Mrs Garwick, who wears really thick glasses, hadn't seen him.

I distracted her attention by pretending to be sick in the back of the van.

She turned round, alarmed, and we sped past Dad.

Three hours later Dad staggered into town, hot, dusty and exhausted.

His shoulders drooped and he blinked painfully when he saw us sitting on the swings under a tree in the Memorial Park.

"Gold, gold, gold for Australia!" we yelled.

"Why didn't you stop for me?" croaked Dad.

Me and Sharon gave each other a puzzled frown.

"We thought you wanted to complete the distance on foot," I said.

"Complete the distance!" shrieked Dad. "It's forty kilometres."

"Forty-two point nine," I said, hanging a gold bottle top round his neck. "Let's hear it for Dad, gold medal winner in the Olympic marathon!"

That was the last Olympic gold medal anyone in our family won.

We're all glued to the telly, though, watching the real gold medals being won in Atlanta.

All except Dad.

He's gone to stay with Uncle Wal.

"Now That's What
I Call Spooky"

BY

KAYE UMANSKY

Illustrated by Curtis Jobling

"Now That's What I Call Spooky"

It was a black, black night up at the haunted castle. The wind howled, the rain lashed and the thunder and lightning elbowed their way through the clouds.

"Hear that?" said the Skeleton. "Shockin' weather for this time of year, innit?"

He was sitting at a small table in the great hall with two companions. All three were playing cards by the light of a single candle.

"Sssh!" snapped the second player crossly. "Art thou playing cards, or what?"

The second player was see-through and came in two bits: Head and Body. The Head sat on a crisp ruff on the table. The matching Body sat hunched on a chair, and held the cards with great difficulty because of its transparent hands.

"I'm just sayin' it's shockin' for April," repeated the Skeleton. "Right, Nev?" he appealed to the third of them, an Empty Suit of Armour.

"You can say that again," agreed the Empty Suit of Armour sitting opposite. "Dunno what to wear, do you? I mean, yesterday on the battlements I left off me gauntlets, right? An' tonight I'm back in 'em again. Perishin' it was up there."

"Yeah. Shockin'," agreed the Skeleton, sucking on a hollow tooth mournfully. "For April."

"As for the lightnin'!" persisted the

Empty Suit of Armour, "I'm a natural target, right? Up on them battlements with all this metal."

"It's no picnic down in the dungeons either," remarked the Skeleton. "Terrible damp. Rats the size of poodles."

"SNAP, by the powers!" shouted the Head suddenly.

"What?" said the Skeleton.

"Snap, I say!" crowed the Head. "Look! Two identical Death-the-Grim-Reapers. Thy cards art now mine!"

The Body reached over and tried to pick up the Skeleton's cards. As usual, they slithered through the Body's foggy fingers.

"Zounds!" hissed the Head. "I HATE that."

"But I weren't lookin'!" protested the Skeleton, gathering up his spilled cards protectively with boney hands. "We'd stopped playin'. I was talkin' about the weather to young Neville 'ere. That's not fair, is it, Nev? Tell him."

"Ho, ho!" chortled the Head. "Canst thou not take losing, eh?"

"It's not that at all!" snapped the Skeleton. "Anyway, I don't believe them cards was both Death-the-Grim-Reapers. One of 'em was that little Demon in pink dungarees. It weren't Snap at all. You're a cheat."

"How dare you!" thundered the Head. The Body leapt to its feet and tried to bring its fist down on the table. It went straight through.

"Anyway, I'm bored with cards," sulked the Skeleton. "That's all we've done for the last five hundred years. Wish we had someone to haunt. Don't you, Neville?"

But the Empty Suit of Armour wasn't listening. He had clanged to his feet, and his visor was cocked to one side.

"Sssssh!" he hissed. "Listen! Footsteps approachin'!"

Sure enough, mixed in with the storm was the sound of slow, measured footsteps on gravel.

"What do you reckon?" said the Skeleton excitedly. "Poor weary traveller lost 'is way in the storm?"

"Hmmm..." The Empty Suit of Armour sounded doubtful. "Bit positive for a poor weary traveller. Poor weary traveller's footsteps usually sound a bit staggery, like."

"Sssh! I'm trying to listen! And get out of my way, Bonesy, I can't see a thing through thy pelvis!" hissed the Head irritably. The Body reached down, gently picked it up and tucked it reassuringly underneath its arm.

At that point the footsteps stopped. There was a pause.

Then three loud knocks sounded on the great door.

The three friends rose to their feet.

"Get ready to scare 'im to death!" said

the Empty Suit of Armour, lifting the heavy latch. The old door swung open with a sinister squeak. At exactly the same time, there came another crash of thunder. And outside...

...Outside stood a tall, mysterious figure holding a strange flat box. Lightning glittered off his polished helmet. He spoke from behind a transparent visor.

"One extra-large, super-duper supreme special with tangy tomato, yummy mozzarella, spicy pork, green pepper and extra cheese, said the stranger. "That'll be nine pounds and forty-five pence, please gents."

There was a long pause. The Head, the Skeleton, and the Empty Suit of Armour looked at each other blankly.

"I didn't order a pizza," said the

Skeleton quietly, looking extra pale.

"Me neither," said the Empty Suit of Armour hollowly.

"Nor me," said the Head with a gulp. The Body gave a little shiver. It was true No-one had ordered it.

"Now THAT'S what I call spooky!" said the Skeleton.

BETWEEN DOGS

BY

HILARY McKAY

Illustrated by Paul Howard

BETWEEN DOGS

Patrick had a dog. A spaniel called Bumper. A dog, thought Patrick, with a coat as golden as sunlight. And then in the autumn, Bumper died.

At first Patrick felt that he would rather be dead like his dog than alive without him. Then that feeling wore off and Patrick had to accept he'd never see Bumper again. That feeling was even worse. It was so final, so never-in-the-world would his dog be there again, but it passed at last and then Patrick simply became a boy without a dog.

By this time people had stopped being quite so sorry for him. After all, they pointed out, Bumper had been an old dog and had had a happy life. Patrick was not the first boy to lose a dog and meanwhile bedrooms must be tidied, bikes put away and homework remembered. Life, in fact, must go on. And Patrick's strange inability to eat the last bit of any biscuit (which had always been Bumper's) or even close a door properly (because Bumper had hated closed doors) must end.

"I need a dog," Patrick said to his father. "I don't feel right without a dog."

Patrick's father said it was the wrong time of year to buy a dog. "It would be a back-end pup!" he told Patrick, meaning an autumn dog, born at the back end of the year. "You don't want a back-end pup! They're lazy! They sit by the fire all day! Wait till the spring and we'll see."

"I need a dog now," said Patrick, but no dog appeared. Not for his birthday, nor for Christmas, nor when he had terrible flu and everything possible was being done to cheer him into recovery. In the end he stopped asking, but the feeling of being incomplete did not stop. It was exactly as if he was not quite Patrick. Like someone else pretending to be Patrick. Like acting all the time.

After the terrible flu Patrick gave up

the acting. He ceased being the not-quite-real Patrick without a dog and became himself again. He stopped forcing himself to eat the ends of biscuits and took to stowing them in his pockets instead. If he found a perfect stick for a dog to chase he picked it up and let himself feel pleased, and when a suitable throwing place arrived, he threw it quite cheerfully. In the supermarket he hovered by the dog food cans instead of hurrying past with averted eyes and chose for his dog the most delicious-sounding, regardless of price. He began to feel much better. It was as if the dog he owned was very close, but just out of sight.

Quite often, lying in bed, he seemed to hear him. The sound of water being lapped in a different room, pattering feet in the hall, the scrape of a door being pushed across the carpet, once a sneezing bark.

Then there came a night when Patrick emerged from layers of drowsy sleep and all the empty weeks were forgotten. He had rolled over and called out, "Bumper!" before he remembered that Bumper could not be there. After that it happened quite often.

Patrick's parents also noticed that there seemed to be an invisible dog haunting the house. They watched Patrick anxiously, not realising that he was quite all right. Almost all right. All right except for the waiting nights when his dog was so certainly in the room with him, and yet Patrick could never quite gather his courage to reach out his hand or open his eyes to look.

"Coward!" Patrick told himself when once again the moment passed and the chance was lost. Still, every night the fear grew less and the temptation grew stronger, until the time came when, waking from deep sleep, he plainly heard his bedroom door being pushed open.

"Bumper," he whispered with his eyes tight shut, as he heard hesitant footsteps patter across the room towards him.

"Bumper," he said and his heart pounded. "Oh, Bumper!" he sobbed, and a moment later there was a rustle and a jolt, the soft heavy weight of a dog beside him on the quilt and silky fur beneath his fingers. "Hello, Bumper," murmured Patrick, and then suddenly, with his face buried in the familiar lovely warmth, he fell asleep.

"Bumper!" he exclaimed as he woke again and it was daylight.

"Not Bumper," said a voice. His

mother's voice. There she was, hovering in the doorway with his father. "Not Bumper, Patrick. Choose another name."

Then for the first time Patrick realised that it was morning. Morning, and a black spaniel puppy was squirming on the bed. Black and perfect, and so absorbing that it was a while before Patrick remembered the dog he had glimpsed through his early morning tears.

How long ago had that been? Seconds or hours? Patrick did not know and could not guess. All he knew for certain was that its coat had not been black, but golden. Golden as sunlight, thought Patrick.

CARNIVAL

BY

GILLIAN CROSS

Illustrated by Mark Longworth

CARNIVAL

The tall man from across the road was outside Bernadine's house, looking at the notice in the window:

FINAL CARNIVAL MEETING
HERE!!!
TONIGHT AT 7.30PM
ALL WELCOME
IF YOU CARE – BE THERE!!!

"I'm going to be the firebird!" Bernadine said. She was so excited that she kept telling people.

The man scowled through his dark glasses. "Carnivals are noisy and disorderly."

Bernadine pulled a face at him and dodged past, heading for her back door. The meeting was about to start and the kitchen was crammed with people. Bernadine's mother was waving her cassette recorder above her head.

"I'm taping you all! So I know who's promised what!"

Everyone laughed. As she switched it on, the back door opened. In stalked the man in dark glasses. Why had he come? Bernadine stared at him.

"Manners!" her mother hissed.

Her father nudged her. "Don't gawp. Go round to Stevie's and fetch your costume."

The firebird costume! Forgetting the man in dark glasses, Bernadine slipped through the back door. As she closed it behind her, all the noise in the kitchen stopped. Which was odd, because Carnival meetings were *never* quiet. She peered through the glass, to see what was happening.

Everyone in the kitchen was very still, gazing at the tall man. Slowly, he took off his dark glasses. His eyes were strange. Sea green and luminous.

"You are all very tired," he murmured – and suddenly everyone started yawning. *Weird*, Bernadine thought. She would have stayed to see what happened, but she couldn't wait. She wanted to be at her cousin Stevie's house, trying on the firebird costume. Who cared about Dark Glasses?

When she came back, the house was silent. She opened the back door and found the kitchen was empty, except for her parents.

"What's up?" she said. "Did the Carnival meeting finish early?"

"There will not be a Carnival," her mother said, in a dull, flat voice.

"*What?*"

Her father nodded. "No bands. No processions. No dancing in the street." His voice was the same. "Carnivals are unimportant and wasteful."

Bernadine stared. "No Carnival?"

"There will not be a Carnival," her parents said together. "No bands. No processions. No dancing in the street. Carnivals are unimportant and wasteful."

That was all they would say. The same words, over and over again. Bernadine went to bed, but she was too miserable to sleep.

At one o'clock in the morning, she

suddenly remembered the cassette recorder. Slipping out of bed, she crept into the kitchen and found it. When she'd rewound the tape, she turned the volume down and pressed PLAY.

Faintly, she heard laughing and joking. Then an abrupt silence. Then the voice of the man in dark glasses.

You are all very tired...

What was he up to?

Suddenly, his voice changed. *You will all do what I say,* he snapped. *Do you understand?*

We understand. Everyone who answered sounded dull and mechanical – like Bernadine's parents. She shuddered.

There will not be a Carnival, the tall man said. *No bands. No fancy dress. No processions. No dancing in the street. Carnivals are unimportant and wasteful.*

The mechanical voices repeated his words.

Bernadine sat down, feeling weak. She knew now what had happened. He'd hypnotised them, to stop the Carnival.

But what was she going to do?

She sat and thought, for an hour. By

the time she went back to bed, she had a plan.

Next day, at school, everyone was miserable.

"'*There will not be a Carnival*'," Stevie growled. "That's all my dad would say."

His friend Nathan nodded. "'*No dancing in the street. Carnivals are unimportant and wasteful*'."

Stevie sighed. "Looks as if you'll miss out on being the firebird, Bern."

"No, I won't!" Bernadine tossed her head. "We can get the Carnival ready without our parents. We know what we have to do!"

"We can decorate the lorries," Nathan said. "And set up the loudspeakers. But we can't drive, or play the music."

Bernadine smiled, mysteriously. "Leave

that to Stevie and me." She beckoned Stevie away from everyone else. "Think you can edit this?" she murmured...

And she took out the tape.

On Carnival Day, Bernadine pulled on the firebird costume and ran downstairs.

Her father frowned. "There will not be a Carnival— "

"Yes there will," Bernadine said.

Dodging her mother, who tried to grab her, she slipped outside. All along the street, other children in fancy dress were dodging their parents, too. Bernadine waved across the road, signalling to Stevie. He started his tape and Bernadine's voice boomed from the loudspeakers:

"CARNIVAL!"

She looked across the street, at the tall man's house. *Come on!* she thought.

CARNIVAL! boomed the tape.

An upstairs window opened across the street. The man in dark glasses looked out scornfully.

"You have wasted your time decorating those lorries," he said. "There will not be a Carnival." He took off his glasses.

Stevie glanced at Bernadine, but she shook her head. *Not yet.*

The man stared down at the crowd for a moment. Then he opened his mouth. "Listen!" he snapped.

Everyone turned to look at him, and Bernadine nodded to Stevie. *Now!*

Stevie switched on. As the man began speaking, his voice was drowned by – itself. From every loudspeaker blared the words he'd spoken at the meeting. Edited by Stevie.

THERE WILL... BE A CARNIVAL...
BANDS... FANCY DRESS... PROCESSIONS...
DANCING IN THE STREET.

The man glared at Bernadine. She could see he was speaking louder, but it was no use. The deafening loudspeakers went on trumpeting his voice.

CARNIVALS ARE... IMPORTANT.

All along the street, grown-ups were fetching out their Carnival costumes. Or starting up lorries. Or seizing musical instruments.

THERE WILL... BE A CARNIVAL...

With a blare of brass and an explosion of dancing, the Carnival procession set off. The tall man slammed his window shut, in disgust, and Bernadine grinned. Then she danced off after the band.

The most joyful firebird the Carnival had ever seen.

JUST WHAT I
ALWAYS WANTED

BY

STEVE MAY

Illustrated by Tania Hurt Newton

Just What I Always Wanted

You know what it's like. Granny and Grandad. They send you something for Christmas, and by Boxing Day you can't remember what it was, let alone where it is. Then, the nightmare: a month later they're coming to visit. In fact, they're arriving any minute. This minute.

Mum says: "I hope you've still got their present. You'd better play with it while they're here."

The doorbell chimes. Gulp!

Don't get me wrong. Granny and Grandad, they're great. They're young and smart and sharp. Too sharp, sometimes.

"Hello, Tom." Big kiss and lipstick.

"Hello, Tom." Bone-crusher handshake.

We're all milling around in the hall.

"My how you've grown," says Gran.

"Not too grown-up for the present we sent, I hope?" says Grandad.

"No, of course not," says Mum.

"He plays with it every day," adds Dad, going red.

"Good!" says Granny. "I thought it might be a bit old-fashioned."

"Never!" smiles Grandad. "The old toys are always the best." They gaggled into the lounge. I went scooting upstairs.

I looked everywhere. Under my bed, behind my desk. I found an old computer game, two dinosaurs, a book token, three odd socks and a pen that leaked all over the carpet. No present. All the time, I'm trying to remember: was it small, wrapped

tight? Was it big, loads of paper?

Mum's calling: "Tom, time to eat!"

I went down.

"Tom's not eating much, is he?" says Granny.

"You want to get away from us old fogies, don't you?" smiles Grandad.

My face is burning.

"He's dying to go and play with your

present," says Mum.

Grandad laughs: "Well, I wouldn't mind seeing it in action while we're here."

Granny laughs too: "Peter, you're nothing but a big child yourself."

Dad is not looking happy: "I'm afraid we can't, not tonight."

Mum gives him a look" "Why ever not?"

Dad tuts: "Because I want to show Mum and Dad the garden."

Mum splutters with laughter: "In the pitch black?"

That gave me an idea: the shed. Stuff gets moved out there if there's nowhere else to put it. It's like magic, the shed: a little pond of yellow light in the darkness.

I found the present straightaway. It was standing large as life on Dad's workbench: shiny red metal and gold bits.

I was too relieved to wonder how it got there. As soon as I saw it, I remembered unwrapping it on Christmas Day, and thinking, what is it? And meaning to try it out, but I never got round to it. Now, before I could have a good look, the door swung open.

"Hello, young man!" Grandad. Behind him, Granny and Mum and Dad. Grandad's rubbing his hands. "Now all we need is to fire it up."

I was fumbling with the thing, trying to find out what it did. Grandad bustled over, took it from me.

Then the smile disappeared from his face. "Oh," he said. "The drive belt's broken."

Mum starts tutting. "Tom, how many times have I told you to be more careful..."

Dad interrupts her. "It wasn't Tom."

"Who was it then?" Granny says. "I've a pretty shrewd idea."

Grandad is smiling again, turns to Dad. Dad holds his hands up, like surrender. "Fair cop. It was me. When I was young, I always wanted one. I couldn't resist trying it out."

Granny shakes her head. "Trust you." She turns to me. "Every toy your father had, he broke."

I said, "But we're going to mend it, aren't we? And it is really, really good."

And we did fix it, and it was really, really good.

Later, back indoors, Grandad said, "Next time, we'll know.

"Know what?" asked Mum.

"Know to buy two," laughed Granny, "so they can have one steam engine each."

THE LEX FILES

BY

ROBERT SWINDELLS

Illustrated by Jolyon Webb

THE LEX FILES

I want to get one thing straight before we start. Me and James Otterbury aren't posh just because we're at boarding school, right? It's called The Cordwainers School and it's full of ordinary kids, including us. Me and James are a *little* bit famous now because of the skeleton, but before that, James held the school belching record and I could spit into a burger box from ten paces and that's all. Ordinary kids.

Every boarding school has its ghost and ours is no exception. Our ghost is a kid. It's known as the sad boy because everybody who's seen it says it looks really, really sad. Loads of people have seen it. The caretaker. The nurse. About a million kids, including me and James. No one's *spoken* to it though, except the two of us, and I don't think anybody'll get the chance now. If you're not doing anything special I'll tell you all about it, but I must warn you, it's weird. *Seriously* weird.

It's Thursday afternoon. D.T. with Ms Wheelwright. As we walk in she says, "James Otterbury, fetch the spare workbench from the cellar. Go with him, Sophie Milburn."

So, off we trot, the pair of us, along the dim corridor and down the old stone stairs. We're not thinking about ghosts at all because it's the middle of the afternoon and the sun's shining outside, but as we cross the cellar, James stops dead and says, "Listen."

I listen, and it's somebody crying. I don't know if you've ever heard crying where there's an echo, but I can tell you it sounds a lot sadder than ordinary crying

I look at James. "Who do you think it is?" Part of me's going, *the sad boy.* Another part says, *no way.*

"How the heck do I know?" whispers James. "A first year I suppose, feeling homesick. It's coming from the far cellar, through the arch where nobody ever goes."

The school's two hundred years old and teachers have been dumping stuff in that far cellar since the eighteenth century. You should see it. Anyway, it's coming from there and we creep in. The main cellar's got electric light, but if this one has, we can't find a switch.

James is right. It's a first year. He's

sitting on an ancient stool, up to his knees in junk and with his head in his hands.

I was homesick in Year One and feel really sorry for him. I say, "Missing your mum?"

He nods in his hands.

"What's your name?"

"Billings. Alexander Heracles Billings."

"Good grief. All right if we call you Lex?"

Another nod.

"It gets better, Lex. Everybody's homesick at first. Anyway, it's the hols in three weeks."

I'm looking at the kid's clothes. Something not quite right.

He sniffles, talks into his palms. "Hols're no use to me. I'm stuck here. Forever."

Then it hits me, of course. *The sad boy*. I look at James. "It's— "

"I know, the sad boy." He looks at the ghost. "*Why* are you stuck here?"

"'Cause my bones're here."

"Your b... *bones*?"

"Yes"

"How come?"

And Alexander Heracles Billings takes his hands away from his face and tells us this story.

"*It's 1940 and England's at war. There's bombing. The school's too close to the city so they decide to move it.*"

"Move the school?"

"*Not the building, you ass. The teachers. The children. To a big house in the country. It's forty miles away. Too far for my people to visit at weekends as they do here. I'm homesick as it is. I don't want to go, so when everybody's milling about with labels and parents and gas-masks and packets of sandwiches, I slip away. Creep down here. Hide. Oh, I don't expect to get away with it. Can't think of anything else to do, that's all. I expect them to come searching but they don't. There are voices*" *for a while. The sound of engines, then quiet. I'll wait till dusk, then make my way home. They won't send me away, I tell myself. Not when they see how unhappy I am. But at dusk, I find somebody's shut and locked the big iron gate at the top of the steps. I call out. Yell at the top of my voice. The echo scares me silly. I think they'll notice the other end. Notice I'm not there. That they've left me behind. Somebody will come.*

But nobody did, because two days later something horrible happened. The big house in the country – the new Cordwainers School – received a direct hit from a stray bomb. It was a big bomb, the sort they called a Satan, and it practically destroyed the house. Most of my friends – it was an all boys' school then – were killed, and everybody assumed I was among them. So... " He shrugged. "*Here I stayed till starvation finished me. My friends - they're all with their mums and dads now, but I can't go to mine because—*"

"Because what?" I murmured.

"Because my bones aren't buried. They're over there, in the corner behind that great cabinet. I could show you if you like."

And he did. And then he faded out, and me and James went and told Ms Wheelwright. She didn't believe a word. Marched us off to old Chocky's office. His real name's Mr Barr and he's the Head. Turned out he'd *heard* of Alexander Heracles Billings. School records.

So off we all go to the cellar and me

and James show Chocky what's behind the cabinet and that's that.

Old Lex gets a decent burial and me and James get new nicknames. I'm Agent Skull, he's Agent Moulder. The kids talk about The Lex Files. I hope he knows what's they're on about, old Lex. I hope he's having a good laugh with his mum and dad in that place where the hols go on forever.

THE TRAVELLER

BY

THERESA BRESLIN

Illustrated by Mark Robertson

THE TRAVELLER

"It's on nights like this," said the old man, "with blizzards from the north, that a traveller can lose his way."

"You think that's what happened? All those years ago?" the innkeeper asked.

"Who knows?" said the old one. "Perhaps he sank in a drift. Perhaps murder was done." He held out his wine cup. "But it was on just such a night as this, with heavy snow cloud building in the Northlands, and the wind driving sleet before it, that my Traveller arrived."

The innkeeper tilted the jug as the old man began his tale.

"The sun had barely set when a great raging snowstorm swept down into this valley." The storyteller looked towards the door. Outside the gale shrieked and tore at the roof tiles. "Like tonight." He lowered his voice. "Mark my words well, now. Just like this very night," he whispered.

All in the alehouse drew close as the old man continued. "Just as the storm was at its wildest, the inn door crashed open and a man stood there."

As the old man stopped for breath, the door of the inn flew open and slammed back as the wind took it. "Mercy save us!" he cried, and made the sign to ward off the evil one.

"Tush," said the innkeeper. "'Tis only another traveller. Come up to the fire, boy."

The youth walked to the inglenook and, keeping his cloak wrapped about him, he sat down and stretched long legs out before the flames.

The old man gazed at the boy, with rheumy eyes. "Another traveller?" he muttered. "Strange…"

"Aye, and it was strange that night, sixteen years ago, by all accounts," prompted one of the company.

The old man returned to his wine and his story. "Now this Traveller who stood in the doorway was a tall man with eyes of sharp blue, and a grim purpose in his manner.

'I saw your light,' he said, 'and stopped to ask the way.'

'From where have you come?' I asked him.

'South.'

'Then South is where you must return.' I said. 'There is no way on from here. Eastwards is the sea, and to the North the mountain passes are blocked until late springtime.'

Then the Traveller grasped my arm. 'And what lies West?'

I shook my head. 'Nothing but ill lies to the West,' I said."

"Aye truly," interrupted one of the old man's cronies. "As it is today."

The innkeeper spat on the floor. "A curse to the Lord of Aeleslan, murderer and widow maker."

From under the hood of his cloak, the boy by the fire turned his head to listen.

"It was as bad then, as now," said the old man. "Taxes and rents few could afford. Evictions and hangings for those who could not pay. And, as I told him, the

Traveller slumped down in the seat by the hearth."

The old man paused and glanced at the boy sitting in the shadow of the great chimney.

"I explained that old Lord Aeleslan had died one year since. And that his son, banished for his foul deeds and evil ways, had returned from exile on his father's death, bringing a young wife. And how we had hoped that she – beautiful and good as she was – would change him. But she was a fragile flower. He kept her prisoner in his keep, and recently, when she had borne the son he craved, he left her to die.

At that, the Traveller started from his chair. 'She is dead then?' he cried. 'You are sure of this?'

I nodded, and he fell back into his seat.

After a long moment he looked up at me. 'And what of the child?' he asked.

'Healthy and well... for now...' I replied, 'but left in the care of that wicked man, poison will soon flow in those veins too.'

Then my Traveller got to his feet. 'I must go now to the House of Aeleslan,' he said. He went to the inn door. Outside, the shroud of the night was bleak and bitter. I tried to stop him. 'Hold off until dawn. Your business with the Lord Aeleslan can wait until morning.'

The Traveller looked at me, and spoke softly. 'The business I have to do,' he said, 'is best done in the dark.'"

The old man's voice was very low as he finished his tale.

"He went out into the darkness and we never saw him again."

"Nor hear aught of him?" The question came from the youth by the fire.

The old man started at the sound of the voice, and turned to reply.

"We heard that he entered the House of Aeleslan, but he did not kill the oppressor. Instead… he stole the child."

There was a sharp breath from the youth. "Did they pursue him?" he asked.

"He was hunted day and night but never found. They say he must have tried for a way through the mountains and if that is true, then he surely perished. Things have gone from bad to ill these sixteen years. Starving men caught snaring rabbits in his woods lie rotting in the keep of Aeleslan."

"Yet it was wrong to take the child as revenge," said one of the listeners. "An innocent babe died because the Traveller loved the mother and lost her to another."

"No," the youth by the fire spoke again. "The child was taken for love, not revenge. The love that a brother bears his sister caused your Traveller to carry the child to safety through the Northern passes. She had sent word to him to rescue her from her madman husband, and he came as swiftly as he could... too late.

"Too late for her, but…" and then the boy by the fire got up and unwrapped his cloak, "…but not for me," he said.

And the youth stood tall, with a proud face and deep-set blue eyes. "On my uncle's death I found her letter to him, and I knew where to seek my past."

He gathered his cloak and went towards the door. "By morning, I promise you, there will be only one prisoner in the Keep of Aeleslan."

"Wait!" cried the old man. "It will be safer to hold off until dawn,"

The youth turned in the doorway and smiled. "The business I have to do," he said quietly, "is best done in the dark."

THE DOG SNATCHER

BY

PETE JOHNSON

Illustrated by Nick Sharratt

THE DOG SNATCHER

Now, I don't go around dognapping. But this dog was just getting on my nerves. I mean, it wanted attention all the time.

"It's crying again," said Suzy, my best friend.

"So what," I replied.

"Claire, how can you be so cruel?"

"Very easily. And it's not crying, it's beeping."

But Suzy wasn't listening. She was busy with her cyberdog. It's like nothing else matters. And that dog beeps every five seconds. I'm not joking.

Last week, we went to the cinema. The film was just starting when 'beep, beep, beep' came from Suzy's pocket. The couple next to us started hissing furiously.

Suzy was indignant. "But he only wanted to let me know he'd done a poo, poo."

I was so pleased when cyberpets were banned from our school. At last, I thought, I'll get some peace. But Suzy just smuggled the dog in the bottom of her satchel.

Whenever our teacher, Mr Francis, wasn't looking she'd have her nose in it. She was getting more and more addicted. I had to do something.

Then, one day at school it kept refusing to eat. It stood behind the glass, shaking its head. All morning Suzy fussed over it. Finally, it went to sleep.

"Just leave it now," I said.

Even Suzy looked a bit fed up. "I think I will," she said slipping the dog back into her satchel.

A moment later, Mr Francis called Suzy into his room. She rushed away leaving her satchel behind. This was my chance to do a bit of dog snatching. So I did. I threw the dog into my locker.

"If you make a sound I'll smash you into tiny bits," I snarled. "And, that's a promise."

Mr Francis had told Suzy she must work harder. She was always too busy with her cyberpet to do any homework. That afternoon Suzy thought her dog was sleeping peacefully and didn't check on him once.

After school, she rushed off home, determined to catch up on her missing homework. I took the dog out of my locker. I planned to throw it away when walking home. But I didn't. Instead, I hid it down the back of our settee. I'd get rid of it later.

Then Suzy rang. She'd discovered her dog was missing; her mum was driving her back to school to search for it. I felt so guilty. But then I thought of all the time Suzy would waste on that dog. Really, I was saving her hundreds of hours.

Later, I was watching telly with my mum. We were laughing at *Neighbours*, when Mum suddenly shot up into the air as if she'd just been bitten.

"There's something in that settee," she hissed. "Listen."

Of course you know exactly what I heard.

"Don't worry, Mum," I said, "it's only

a silly toy." I rushed out with the dog to the kitchen, then I flung it in the bin.

That night I woke up to hear a very familiar sound – beeping. It was really loud, too. I sat up in bed afraid my parents might hear it. But no-one else stirred. I put my head under the pillows. If anything, the beeping sounded louder.

I crept downstairs. I was going to throw the dog into the back garden, where it could rot away. I reached into the bin. My hand touched the remains of some baked beans. Yuk! Then I snatched up the cyberdog.

I glared at it.

The dog had its head right up against the glass. There was a skull at the bottom of the screen. This meant it needed medicine urgently.

"Beep, beep," it cried piteously.

"You'll be lucky," I said.

"Beep, beep." Its cries were growing fainter. Soon it would be gone.

Suddenly, I pressed the button and gave it some medicine. Don't ask me why. Then I fed it. He was starving.

For the rest of the night it slept on the little table beside my bed.

In the morning, I fed it again, then gave it some exercise to make sure it didn't get too fat. I even cleaned up its poo, poo. I felt very ashamed. I decided I would return the dog to Suzy straight away. It wasn't too annoying. Not when you got to know it.

I waited for Suzy by the school gates. To my amazement, she was smiling.

"Meet my new cyberpet – a dinosaur."

"But, what about your dog?"

"I'm really glad it disappeared, because Mum's bought me a much better one. It doesn't keep beeping all the time and it can…"

I had to walk away. Well, the dog was only in my pocket. And the poor thing could hear every word, couldn't he?

ACKNOWLEDGEMENTS

The publishers gratefully acknowledge the following for permission to reproduce copyright material in this anthology:

David Higham Associates for *Mackerel and Chips* by Michael Morpurgo © Michael Morpurgo 1995; Maggie Noach Agency for *Little Green Men* by Jean Ure © Jean Ure 1997; David Higham Associates for *The Elephants' Revenge* by Jamila Gavin © Jamila Gavin 1997; Michael Hardcastle for *World Cup Fever* © Michael Hardcastle 1994; David Higham Associates for *Hunt the Baby* by Jacqueline Wilson © Jacqueline Wilson 1995; *Joey and the Dutch Destroyer* by Brian Jacques © Brian Jacques 1996. Reprinted by kind permission of The Abbey Company Limited; Morris Gleitzman for *Olympic Marathon* by Maurice Gleitzman © Creative Input Pty Ltd 1996; Caroline Sheldon Literary Agency for *"Now That's What I Call Spooky"* by Kaye Umansky © Kaye Umansky 1991; Hilary McKay for *Between Dogs* © Hilary McKay 1995 first published in Young Telegraph January 1996; Gillian Cross for *Carnival* © Gillian Cross 1996, first published in Young Telegraph September 1996; Micheline Steinberg Playwrights for *Just What I Always Wanted* by Steve May © Steve May 1996, first published in Young Telegraph January 1996 [Also by Steve May: *Friendly Fire*; *Closer Closer*; *Egghead*; *15, Going on 20*; *How's Harry.*] Jennifer Luithlen Agency for *The Lex Files* by Robert Swindells © Robert Swindells 1997; Laura

Cecil Literary Agency for *The Traveller* by Theresa Breslin © Theresa Breslin 1997; Jennifer Luithlen Agency for *The Dog Snatcher* by Pete Johnson © Pete Johnson 1997. All the stories in this anthology were first published by *Young Telegraph*.

The publishers would like to thank *Young Telegraph* and Two-Can Publishing Limited without whom this anthology would not have been possible.